Bernelly & Harriet

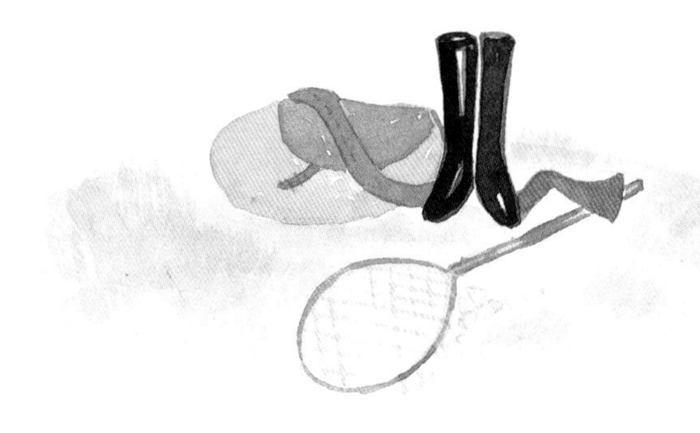

To my wonderful family

To Harriet,
my fairy god southerner

And to David and Rebecca
for believing in my work

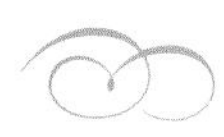

First Edition

Library of Congress Cataloging-in-Publication Data

Dahlie, Elizabeth.
Bernelly and Harriet: the country mouse and the city mouse / by Elizabeth Dahlie. — 1st ed.
p. cm.
Summary: Updates Aesop's fable as Bernelly, a fly-fishing instructor, is introduced to the excitement of city life by her cousin, Harriet, who then accompanies Bernelly to the peaceful countryside in search of artistic inspiration.
ISBN 0-316-60811-4
[1. Fables. 2. Folklore.] I. Country mouse and the city mouse. English. II. Title.
PZ8.2.D23 Be 2002
[398.2]—dc21
[E] 00-048789

10 9 8 7 6 5 4 3 2 1

TWP

Printed in Singapore

The illustrations for this book were done in gouache.
The text was set in Cantoria, and the display type is Liberty.

ELIZABETH DAHLIE

Bernelly & Harriet

THE COUNTRY MOUSE AND THE CITY MOUSE

Little, Brown and Company
Boston New York London

Bernelly was a country mouse. She lived west of the city in a small village that had everything a mouse could need—except a shoe shop.

From spring through fall Bernelly was a fly-fishing instructor. . . .

And in winter she spent her time tying beautiful flies.

One cold, wet day as Bernelly took her morning walk, she noticed something odd. One of her paws was icy and wet. Her boot had sprung a leak! *Oh, bother,* she thought.

Later on, while warming herself by the fire, Bernelly had an exciting idea. *I shall go and see Cousin Harriet in the city. Harriet has been begging me to come for a visit, and I do need a new pair of boots.*

So Bernelly phoned her cousin,

packed her bags,

and was off.

Harriet met Bernelly at the train station. Although they hadn't seen each other since they were wee mice, they knew each other right away.

"Darling-Bernelly-so-good-to-see-you-I-have-missed-you-so," Harriet said all in one breath. "How terribly exciting to take you shoe shopping and show you the sights."

Hand in hand they walked down crooked cobblestone streets to Harriet's apartment.

Harriet was a famous artist, and her home was also her studio. In winter she painted glorious masterpieces. . . .

And in summer she traveled to exotic places that might inspire her.

On the morning after Bernelly's arrival, the two cousins sat down to breakfast and discussed their plans for the day.

"There is so much to see in our fine city. By the time you leave, I'm sure you'll see how far superior city life is to country life," Harriet said quite convincingly.

Harriet took Bernelly to the State House. . . .

They watched the chess players in the park. . . .

They went to the museum. . . .

And they rode the Swan Boats.

Bernelly and Harriet attended the ballet. . . .

And visited Harriet's club.

They traveled exclusively by trolley.

Finally, they went to Harriet's favorite shoe shop . . .

and found just the boots Bernelly was looking for!

But after a long week of shopping and sightseeing, Bernelly was beginning to feel overwhelmed.

So when Harriet asked her if she did not indeed find city life preferable to the country, Bernelly momentarily forgot her manners and snapped, "No!"

Then she explained, "It is just too crowded and noisy here. I miss being able to sit quietly by the river watching my beautiful trout."

"Rrrreally!" exclaimed Harriet. "Well, then I must visit you in the country," she said firmly. "Perhaps it will inspire me."

Bernelly was thrilled. She couldn't wait to show Harriet off to her friends and let the countryside inspire her cousin.

First they went fly-fishing.

Bernelly showed Harriet her favorite flies.

They worked on Bernelly's garden. . . .

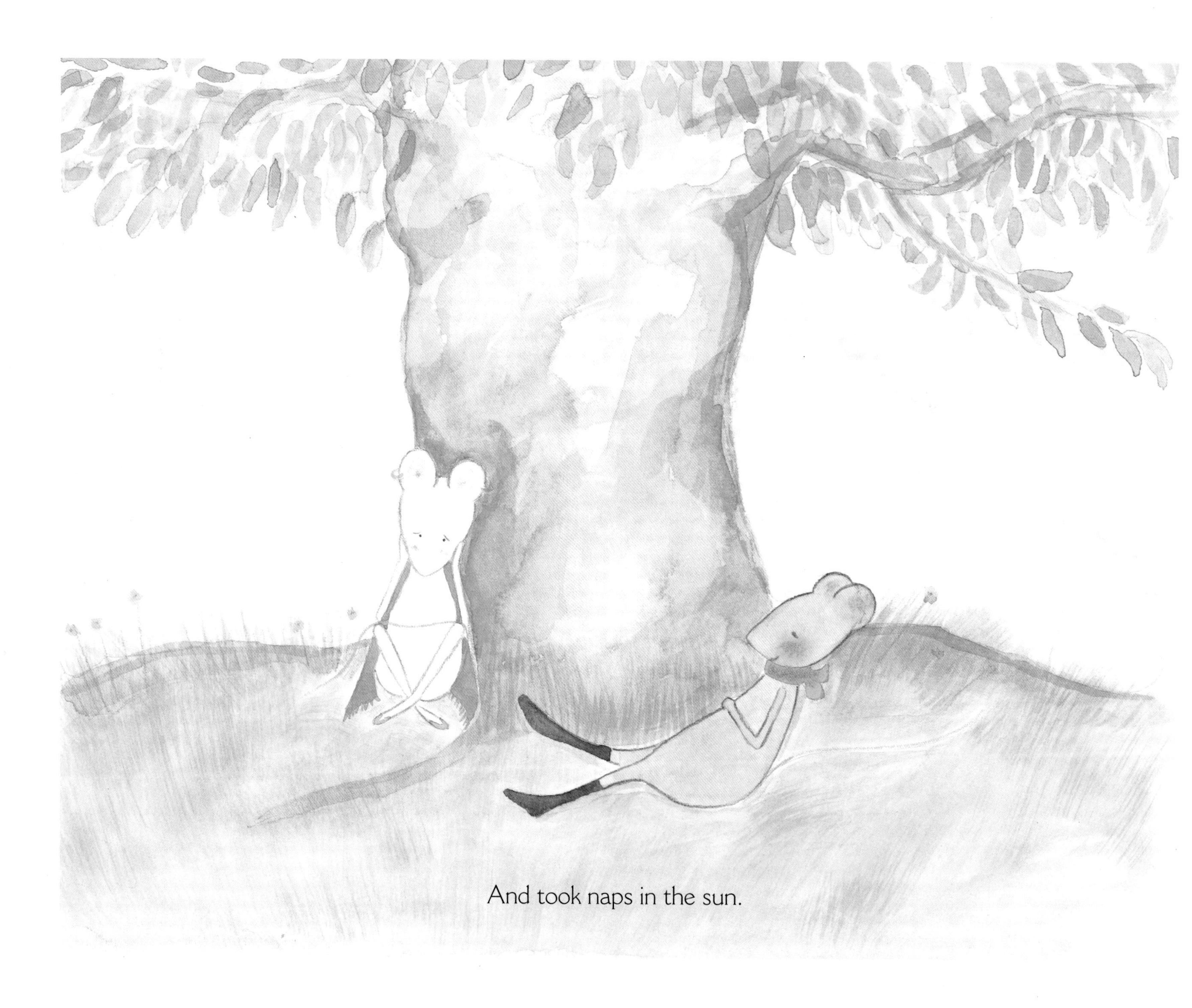

And took naps in the sun.

Bernelly hosted great dinner parties with exciting tales of trout.

Near the end of Harriet's stay, during a long walk, Bernelly eagerly asked Harriet what she thought of country life.

"Darling Bernelly, although the country suits you, it is much too quiet for me. I miss the hustle and bustle of city life — the noise, the smells, the shopping!" said Harriet excitedly.

"Oh, dear," said Bernelly. "Do you mean to say that the countryside hasn't inspired you at all?"

"Oh, it has, it has . . . in its own way," said Harriet quite mysteriously.